Cinderella's Big Foot

Written by Laura North
Illustrated by Martin Remphry

Crabtree Publishing Company
www.crabtreebooks.com

Crabtree Publishing Company
www.crabtreebooks.com
1-800-387-7650

PMB 59051, 350 Fifth Ave.
59th Floor,
New York, NY 10118

616 Welland Ave.
St. Catharines, ON
L2M 5V6

Published by Crabtree Publishing in 2014

For Sue and Michael.
L.N.

Series editor: Melanie Palmer
Editor: Crystal Sikkens
Notes to adults: Reagan Miller
Series advisor: Catherine Glavina
Series designer: Peter Scoulding
Production coordinator and Prepress technician: Margaret Amy Salter
Print coordinator: Margaret Amy Salter

Library and Archives Canada Cataloguing in Publication

North, Laura, author
Cinderella's big foot / written by Laura North ; illustrated by Martin Remphry.

(Tadpoles: fairytale twists)
Issued in print and electronic formats.
ISBN 978-0-7787-0440-9 (bound).--ISBN 978-0-7787-0448-5 (pbk.).-- ISBN 978-1-4271-7560-1 (pdf).--ISBN 978-1-4271-7552-6 (html)

I. Remphry, Martin, illustrator II. Title.

PZ7.N815Ci 2014 j823'.92 C2013-908325-1
C2013-908326-X

First published in 2010 by Franklin Watts (A division of Hachette Children's Books)

Printed in Canada/022014/MA20131220

Library of Congress Cataloging-in-Publication Data

CIP available at Library of Congress

This story is based on the traditional fairy tale, Cinderella, but with a new twist. Can you make up your own twist for the story?

Once upon a time, Cinderella lived with her two evil stepsisters.

They made her wear rags and clean the kitchen all day long.

"Scrub those pots!" said one stepsister. "Clean up this mess," ordered the other.

One day, a gold invitation
to the royal ball arrived.
"Cinderella, you will stay here and
clean while we meet the prince!"
laughed the evil stepsisters.

"I wish I could go to the ball," sobbed Cinderella.

Suddenly, a woman with wings
appeared in a puff of smoke.
"I'm your fairy godmother!"

“Poor Cinderella, you will go to the ball!” she said kindly.

She tapped her wand three times. Cinderella's dirty rags became a beautiful white dress. Her shoes sparkled with diamonds.

Cinderella rushed off to the ball, without thanking her fairy godmother. She had one thing on her mind: the prince.

“The prince will fall in love with me because I am so beautiful!” boasted Cinderella.

All the girls wanted to meet the prince. Cinderella pushed them aside. “He’s mine!” she yelled.

The handsome prince saw Cinderella stomp on one girl's toes and pull another girl's hair.

But the prince fell in love with her anyway. She didn't let anyone else near him! They danced together all night.

Then, as the clock struck midnight, Cinderella's lovely white dress turned back into dirty rags.

She ran away in shame. She was in such a hurry that one of her shoes fell off as she ran!

The next day, there was a loud knock at Cinderella's door. It was the prince!

"My true love lost her shoe," he declared. "I will marry the girl whose foot it fits."

"Get out of my way!" said Cinderella, pushing past her stepsisters. She moved her tiny foot toward the tiny shoe.

Suddenly, there was a BANG and a big puff of smoke. The fairy godmother was back!

"Cinderella!" she said, "you are just as mean as your stepsisters. You don't deserve to marry the prince!"

The fairy godmother tapped her magic wand three times. Cinderella's foot grew...

and grew...

and grew!

Now her foot was too big

for the shoe!

"You've gotten too big for your boots," laughed her stepsisters.

"Oh fairy godmother, I know
I've been bad," wept Cinderella.
"If you shrink my foot back,
I'll never be horrible again."

“Very well,” the fairy godmother replied. “If you promise to be kind, even to your stepsisters.”

A week later, there was a royal wedding. Cinderella kept her word. She invited her stepsisters and even let them be her bridesmaids.

But *they* were just as rude and horrible as before!

Puzzle 1

Put these pictures in the correct order. Which event is the most important? Try writing the story in your own words. Use your imagination to put your own "twist" on the story!

Puzzle 2

1. I must find my true love.

2. I am the most beautiful of all.

3. I can grant your wish.

4. I am holding a royal ball.

5. No one gets in my way!

6. I like to help people in trouble.

Match the speech bubbles to the correct character in the story. Turn the page to check your answers.

Notes for adults

TADPOLES: Fairytale Twists are engaging, imaginative stories designed for early fluent readers. The books may also be used for read-alouds or shared reading with young children.

TADPOLES: Fairytale Twists are humorous stories with a unique twist on traditional fairy tales. Each story can be compared to the original fairy tale, or appreciated on its own. Fairy tales are a key type of literary text found in the Common Core State Standards.

THE FOLLOWING PROMPTS BEFORE, DURING, AND AFTER READING SUPPORT LITERACY SKILL DEVELOPMENT AND CAN ENRICH SHARED READING EXPERIENCES:

1. **Before Reading**: Do a picture walk through the book, previewing the illustrations. Ask the reader to predict what will happen in the story. For example, ask the reader what he or she thinks the twist in the story will be.
2. **During Reading**: Encourage the reader to use context clues and illustrations to determine the meaning of unknown words or phrases.
3. **During Reading**: Have the reader stop midway through the book to revisit his or her predictions. Does the reader wish to change his or her predictions based on what they have read so far?
4. **During and After Reading**: Encourage the reader to make different connections:
   Text-to-Text: How is this story similar to/different from other stories you have read?
   Text-to-World: How are events in this story similar to/different from things that happen in the real world?
   Text-to-Self: Does a character or event in this story remind you of anything in your own life?
5. **After Reading**: Encourage the child to reread the story and to retell it using his or her own words. Invite the child to use the illustrations as a guide.

HERE ARE OTHER TITLES FROM TADPOLES: FAIRYTALE TWISTS FOR YOU TO ENJOY:

Jack and the Bean Pie	978-0-7787-0441-6 RLB	978-0-7787-0449-2 PB
Little Bad Riding Hood	978-0-7787-0442-3 RLB	978-0-7787-0450-8 PB
Princess Frog	978-0-7787-0443-0 RLB	978-0-7787-0452-2 PB
Sleeping Beauty—100 Years Later	978-0-7787-0444-7 RLB	978-0-7787-0479-9 PB
The Lovely Duckling	978-0-7787-0445-4 RLB	978-0-7787-0480-5 PB
The Princess and the Frozen Peas	978-0-7787-0446-1 RLB	978-0-7787-0481-2 PB
The Three Little Pigs and the New Neighbor	978-0-7787-0447-8 RLB	978-0-7787-0482-9 PB

VISIT WWW.CRABTREEBOOKS.COM FOR OTHER CRABTREE BOOKS.

Answers

Puzzle 1

The correct order is: 1e, 2c, 3a, 4d, 5f, 6b

Puzzle 2

Cinderella: 2, 5

The prince: 1, 4

The fairy godmother: 3, 6